W9-ABN-705

Old Manhattan Has Some Farms

E-I-E-I-Grow!

Susan Lendroth

Illustrated by Kate Endle

Charlesbridge

Old Manhattan has some farms.

E-I-E-I-Grow!

On a high-rise here,
in a backyard there—
climbing up, hanging down,
spreading green all over town.

Old Manhattan has some farms.

E-I-E-I-Grow!

Old Atlanta has some worms.

E-I-E-I-Grow!

And with those worms we transform lots.

E-I-E-I-Grow!

Spray some water here,
move an earthworm there—
pull some weeds, grab a spade.
Who's got veggies they can trade?

Old Atlanta has some worms.

E-I-E-I-Grow!

Old Chicago has some roofs.

E-I-E-I-Grow!

And on those roofs are beds of herbs.
E-I-E-I-Grow!

With some basil here
and some mint sprigs there—
pick some chives, add some dill,
string them by our windowsill.

Old Chicago has some roofs.

E-I-E-I-Grow!

And in those hives are busy bees.

E-I-E-I-Grow!

With a buzz-buzz here
and a buzz-buzz there—
pull the frames, spin the wax,
spread some honey on our snacks.

Old Toronto has some hives.

E-I-E-I-Grow!

Old Seattle has some roots.

E-I-E-I-Grow!

And with those roots we don't need dirt.

E-I-E-I-Grow!

With a heat lamp here,
hydroponics there—
arugula, radicchio,
salad greens are great to grow.

Old Seattle has some roots.

E-I-E-I-Grow!

The White House has three compost bins.
E-I-E-I-Grow!

And in those bins we make new dirt.
E-I-E-I-Grow!

With some eggshells here
and some pea pods there—
build the layers, mix a batch,
fertilize the cabbage patch.

The White House has three compost bins.
E-I-E-I-Grow!

Anyone can start a farm.

E-I-E-I-Grow!

And that means you can start one, too.

E-I-E-I-Grow!

Line your pots up here,
shovel dirt in there—
plant your seeds, add some sun.
Yummy crops for everyone!

Together we can all grow food.
E-I-E-I-Grow!

GREEN MATTERS

URBAN FARMS

A farm doesn't need big fields or a barn full of cows and pigs. You can grow food on a very small piece of land, as small as a single pot. Urban farming—growing food in the city—has become popular for many reasons. Plants clean the air and reduce smog. Adding gardens, parks, and trees helps cool a city by a few degrees because soil and plants absorb less heat than streets and buildings. And, of course, the best reason of all for an urban farm is eating all that delicious food!

EMPTY LOTS AND WORMS

Neighborhood groups are transforming empty, trash-filled lots into community gardens. But land where buildings once stood is often packed too hard to grow healthy crops. Adding worms helps. Worms eat organic material in the soil and poop out rich nutrients. Their tunnels loosen the soil, allowing more water and air to reach plant roots. A healthy garden has lots of worms, and gardeners who need more often buy them from worm farms.

Tip: Some gardeners recommend releasing worms in the evening, when it is cooler and fewer birds are out looking for breakfast.

ROOFTOP GARDENS

Buildings in large cities often soar fifty, sixty, even one hundred stories high. People have begun planting container gardens on top of skyscrapers. Herbs like rosemary and basil, and vegetables like tomatoes and peppers, thrive in pots on sunny roofs. Their sweet, spicy scent helps overpower the smell of car exhaust, and local restaurants can serve their fresh produce. Residents of multistory apartment buildings can also grow food high in the sky; pots fit nicely in spaces as small as a balcony or window box.

BEEKEEPING

Whether in backyards or on buildings (including the roof of a Toronto opera house), beehives thrive in urban settings. As the bees gather pollen from flowers around the city, they carry the grains from one plant to another. Pollinating the plants enables fertilization so that fruits and vegetables develop. Hardworking bees also produce honey. To harvest honey from beehives, beekeepers pull the wooden frames of honeycomb from the hive boxes and spin them in machines that force honey from the wax.

HYDROPONICS

Plants can grow in or out of dirt. Minerals in soil dissolve in water, and plants absorb those nutrients through their roots. Mix those same nutrients in liquid, and you can grow plants in that liquid solution without any soil—a system called hydroponics. Add special lights that mimic sunlight, and hydroponic gardens can be grown inside a home.

WHITE HOUSE COMPOST BINS

If you ever have dinner with the president of the United States, your salad greens may come from the White House vegetable garden. To provide rich nutrients for the plants, the White House has three compost bins. Food scraps (but no meat or dairy), grass cuttings, and fallen leaves are layered in the bins along with a little water and soil. Over time the scraps decompose into a rich, organic fertilizer called compost. Gardeners spread compost in the vegetable garden to help the plants grow.

CITY FARMERS

No matter where you live, you can grow food for your family to eat. It's fun to watch seedlings sprout and leaves open. It's even more fun to harvest your crop and serve homegrown fruits and vegetables for dinner. You can start small—a pot of basil on your windowsill—or plant an entire row of lettuce and squash. Take the first step, plant the first seeds, and step back to watch your garden . . . E-I-E-I-Grow!

ADDITIONAL RESOURCES

The Gardening Launch Pad: **www.gardeninglaunchpad.com/kids.html**
A great grab bag of dozens of gardening websites for kids

Inside Urban Green: **www.insideurbangreen.org/kids-gardening/**
An informative blog with practical, easy ideas for gardening in urban settings

KidsGardening, Parent Primer: **www.kidsgardening.org/parent/primer**
A step-by-step guide to engaging children in gardening

Sustainable Urban Gardens: **www.sacgardens.org/gardenKids.html**
A thoughtful selection of children's books, websites, and resources

SINGING "OLD MANHATTAN"

Try singing "Old Manhattan Has Some Farms" using the name of your own city or town. To mimic the song's original rhythm, I chose city names of three syllables with the stress on the second syllable: Man-HAT-tan, Se-AT-tle, Tor-ON-to. Many other cities, such as Columbus, Miami, and Milwaukee, follow the same pattern.

With a few tweaks, cities with different syllable counts also work:

> Two syllables: "Our town HOUSTON has some farms . . ."

> Four syllables: "SAN FRANCISCO has some farms . . ."

> And this line suits just about everyone: "Our hometown has urban farms . . ."

Now let the songs begin!

Old Manhattan Has Some Farms

Based on the traditional song "Old MacDonald Had a Farm"

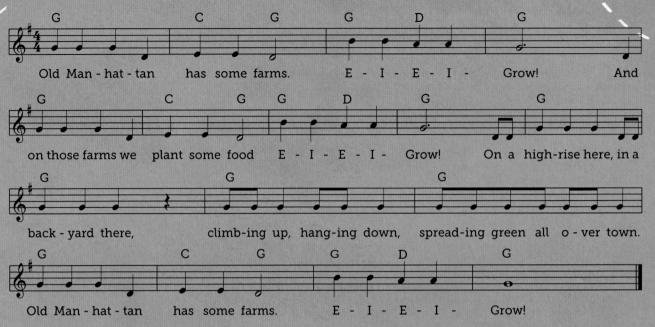

Old Man - hat - tan has some farms. E - I - E - I - Grow! And
on those farms we plant some food E - I - E - I - Grow! On a high-rise here, in a
back - yard there, climb-ing up, hang-ing down, spread-ing green all o - ver town.
Old Man - hat - tan has some farms. E - I - E - I - Grow!

For my aunt Betty, who blooms in every setting—S. L.

To my favorite urban farmers: the Bennett Family of Rockridge Orchards—K. E.

Special thanks to Annie Novak, founder and director of Growing Chefs:
Food Education from Field to Fork, co-founder of the Eagle Street
Rooftop Farm in Brooklyn, New York, and manager of the Edible
Academy at the New York Botanical Garden, for her invaluable
expertise and advice

Text copyright © 2014 by Susan Lendroth
Illustrations copyright © 2014 by Kate Endle
All rights reserved, including the right of reproduction in whole
or in part in any form. Charlesbridge and colophon are registered
trademarks of Charlesbridge Publishing, Inc.

Published by Charlesbridge, 85 Main Street, Watertown, MA 02472
(617) 926-0329 • www.charlesbridge.com

Illustrations painted with Holbein Acryla Gouache on Arches Black
    Cover stock
Display type set in Comic Serif by HVD Fonts
Text type set in Museo Slab by exljbris
Color separations by KHL Chroma Graphics, Singapore
Printed and bound February 2014 by Jade Productions in
    Heyuan, Guangdong, China
Production supervision by Brian G. Walker
Designed by Whitney Leader-Picone

Printed in China
(hc) 10 9 8 7 6 5 4 3 2 1

Library of Congress Cataloging-in-Publication Data
Lendroth, Susan.
    Old Manhattan has some farms: e-i-e-i-grow!/Susan
Lendroth; illustrated by Kate Endle.
    p. cm.
    ISBN 978-1-58089-572-9 (reinforced for library use)
    ISBN 978-1-60734-746-0 (ebook)
    ISBN 978-1-60734-648-7 (ebook pdf)
1. Gardening—Juvenile literature. 2. Urban gardening—
Juvenile literature. I. Endle, Kate. II. Title.
SB457.L46 2014
635.09173'2—dc23   2013014223